noodles®

I LOVE EASTER!

Copyright © 2010 by Hans Wilhelm, Inc.

All rights reserved. Published by Scholastic Inc.
SCHOLASTIC, CARTWHEEL BOOKS, NOODLES, and associated logos
are trademarks and/or registered trademarks of Scholastic Inc.
Lexile is a registered trademark of MetaMetrics, Inc.

Library of Congress Cataloging-in-Publication Data is available.

ISBN: 978-0-545-13476-7

12 11 10 9 8 7 6 5 4 3 2   10 11 12 13 14 15/0

Printed in the U.S.A. 40 • First printing, March 2010

SCHOLASTIC READER
LEVEL 1
50-250 WORDS

I LOVE EASTER!

by Hans Wilhelm

Cartwheel
·B·O·O·K·S·®

SCHOLASTIC INC.
New York   Toronto   London   Auckland
Sydney   Mexico City   New Delhi   Hong Kong

Hooray! It's Easter morning!

Teddy! Let's go on
an Easter egg hunt.

Where are you, Teddy?

Teddy?

Teddy?

I don't see him anywhere.

I will have to hunt
for eggs by myself.

Look!
Here is a red Easter egg!

I found a blue one.

There is a pretty yellow egg.

And here is an egg with lots of stripes.

Now I have a basket full of Easter eggs.
But Teddy isn't here to share them.

I know what I'll do!

I'll share an egg with Scottie.

I'll share one with Cat.

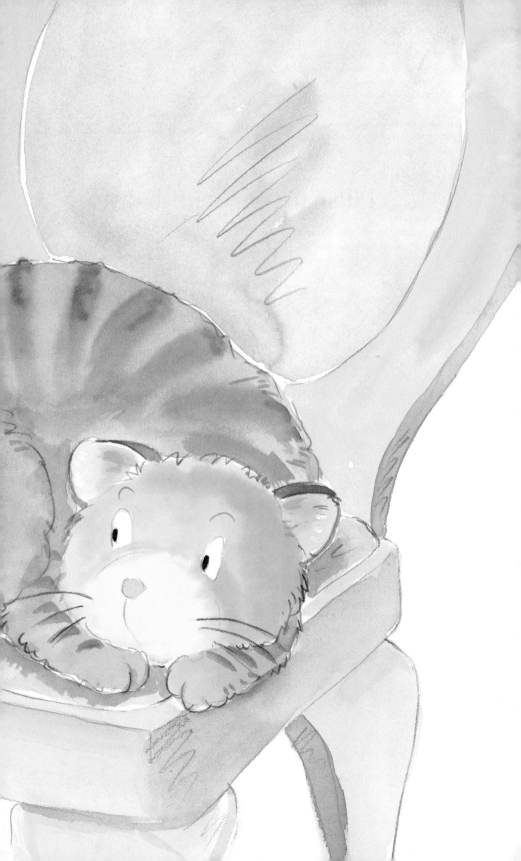

I'll share one with Baby.

Teddy! There you are!

I only have one egg left.
But I'll share it with you.

Happy Easter, Teddy!